This book belongs to

....

....

'For my mother and father, who always read stories
to me when I was a child.' Justin Birch

'For my younger sister Lisa whose favourite joke as
a child was that the Moon was made of cheese, and
for my nieces Hannah and Amber.' Sharon Harmer

This edition printed in 2015 by Alligator publishing Ltd.
Cupcake is an imprint of Alligator Publishing Ltd.
2nd Floor, 314 Regents Park Road, London, N3 2JX

Written by Justin C H Birch
Illustrated by Sharon Harmer

Printed in China 0157

Charlie
and the
Cheesemonster

cupcake

Charlie was bored, so he went to find his Dad.
"Daddy, can we build a rocket please?" asked Charlie.

"Why not?" said his Dad.

They made out of an old sledge, bits from a bicycle, cardboard boxes, a plastic bottle, wire coat hangers, glue and lots of sticky tape. Charlie's Dad found a small motor and when you pressed a button on it, it sounded like the rocket was going to take off. They painted the rocket red and went inside for dinner.

Just before bedtime, the paint was dry, so Charlie and his Dad carried the rocket up to Charlie's bedroom. Charlie's Dad had made Charlie a spaceman's helmet and Charlie wore his spaceman pyjamas and sat in the rocket for his bedtime story.

Then Charlie's parents tucked him into bed, kissed him goodnight and Charlie went to sleep.

A breeze coming in through the open window woke Charlie up.

He looked outside and saw stars and a full Moon shining in the sky. Charlie's rocket glinted in the moonlight, so he put on his helmet and stepped inside.

"Five, four, three, two, one, blast off!"
Charlie pressed the button on the motor.
The noise started, then grew louder and then the rocket
began to move!

It shot straight
out of the open
window!

Whoosh! The rocket swerved upwards and flew high over a tree and kept going. Charlie could see down into his garden and then his whole street.

He shut his eyes and held on tightly for a minute, then opened them. The rocket had risen higher.

All Charlie could see was a blue and green ball that he knew was Planet Earth.

He was a bit scared, but mostly curious, so he kept looking as the Earth grew smaller and smaller.

Bang! There was a big jolt and suddenly the rocket came to a stop.

"Whoops!" shouted Charlie as he got up from the floor of the rocket where he'd fallen.

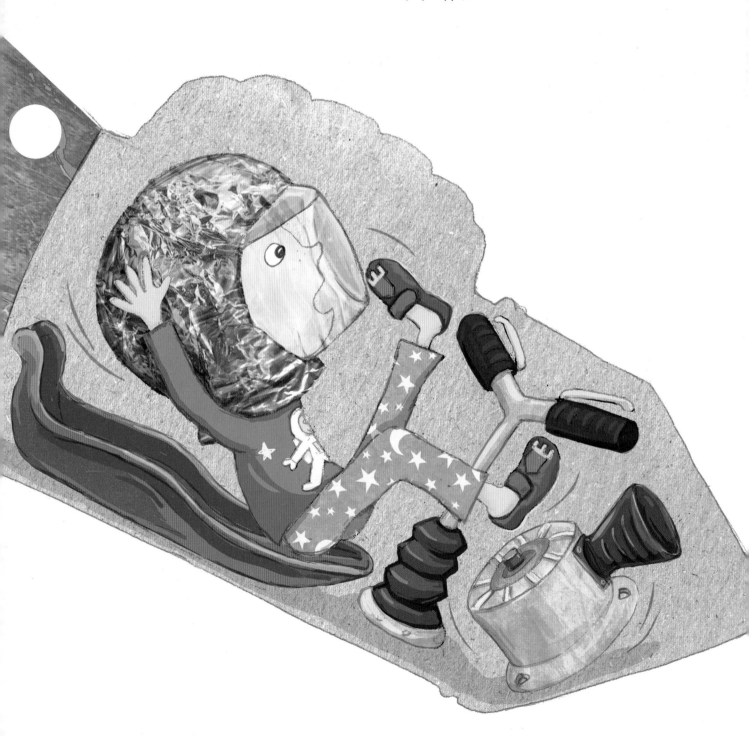

He stepped out of the rocket and looked around.
The ground was creamy white and felt bouncy.

Charlie knelt down and dug his fingers into the surface.
It smelt very familiar. It was his favourite food: Cheddar
cheese! He was on the Moon and it really was made
of cheese!

He took a bite. It was the loveliest cheese he had ever eaten! He was about to have another bite when he heard a noise.

He peered around the side of the rocket. A strange creature was grabbing huge chunks of cheese with its hands and stuffing them into its enormous mouth.

It didn't look scary or unfriendly so Charlie walked up
to it and asked, "Is this the Moon?"
"Yes, this is the moon. What exactly are *you*?" said the
strange creature, as it licked some cheese from its hand.

"Err, I'm a boy," said Charlie.

"A BOY? A BOY?" repeated the creature. "What a strange boy creature you are, so small and pink."

"Errr, so what are *you* then?" asked Charlie.
"I'm a cheesemonster," said the creature. "We eat lots of cheese. It's really tasty. You should try some."

"But you're eating up all of the Moon!" Charlie
blurted out. "That can't be a good thing. What happens
when you've eaten the whole moon? Will you eat my
planet too?" Charlie worried.

The cheesemonster laughed.
"Run out? We can't run out
of cheese! Come with me.
You'll find this interesting."
Charlie's new friend led him
to the dark side of the Moon.

Charlie couldn't believe his eyes. He was looking at the biggest cow he had ever seen, which was being milked by two cheesemonsters.

"This is Millie, our cow. We milk her to make cheese," said the cheesemonster, "Let me explain the cycle of the Moon's cheese to you. . ."

". . .When we eat the cheese, the Moon looks smaller. First we eat the top layer and it looks like someone has taken a slice off the top."

"We keep eating and it looks like a big bite has been taken out of the Moon."

"We carry on eating the
cheese on the bright
side of the Moon,
almost down to the last
slice, so the moon looks
like a tiny crescent."

"Then we take all the
cheese we have made
from the dark side and
put it back on the bright
side. So the Moon looks
new again!"

"So that's why we have
a new moon every Month,"
murmured Charlie.

Charlie had lots of fun with the cheesemonsters.
They let him help make a gigantic block of cheese and
wrote CHARLIE on the side. They put the block on the
top layer of the Moon so that he would see it at bedtime
and they promised not to eat it.

Then they took him back to his rocket and admired it while he got ready to take off.

Charlie counted down from five and pressed the button on the motor. He looked out and waved at the cheesemonsters who waved back and shouted, "Goodbye BOY!"

The rocket zoomed through the air and the
Moon got smaller and smaller. Then there was a rush of
noise and he flew back through his bedroom window and
landed on the floor.

Charlie climbed out of the rocket and
looked up at the fat shining Moon. He was
sure it was a little smaller already.
Yawning, Charlie climbed into bed and fell asleep.

The next morning, the Sun shone and the Moon could just be seen. Charlie grabbed his telescope from the shelf and focused on the Moon.

In the middle of the moon there was a tiny black dot. Charlie tried refocusing but his telescope wasn't strong enough. But he knew that if he could get a stronger telescope he would see that the dot on the Moon was really a name, his name: CHARLIE.

Smiling, Charlie went downstairs to breakfast.
It was cheese on toast.